This book is dedicated to the millions of children around the world, who are all different but yet the same.

Copyright © 2020 by Rayna Best

All rights reserved. No part of this book may be reproduced or used in any manner without written permission of the copyright owner except for the use of quotations in a book review. For more information, address: raynadenise@yahoo.com

Animated Like Me

By
Rayna Best

Sometimes he had so much energy that the other zebras would flee.

He had trouble being still, so much so,
that sometimes he even wiggled his toes.

On tough days, Kamron the zebra had a hard time controlling his noise.

This made him stand out from other little zebra boys.

He was often impatient and did not like waiting his turn. And when it came to new games it was hard for him to learn. He could not help it, no matter how hard he tried.

And on these specific days he would just sit and cry cry cry! "No one likes me!" he would angrily say. "I can't be the only one who feels this way.

One evening Kamron came across another little zebra who was very quiet when she was alone. He befriended her and she became the nicest little zebra he had ever known.

Her name was Kamille and oh was she a thrill. She daydreamed and talked A LOT but to Kamron that was her special skill.

Kamille the zebra was often distracted and sometimes overreacted.

She would throw tantrums all over the land. Sometimes so loud it sounded like a marching band.

But on good days she was as sweet as can be and filled Kamron with so much laughter and glee.

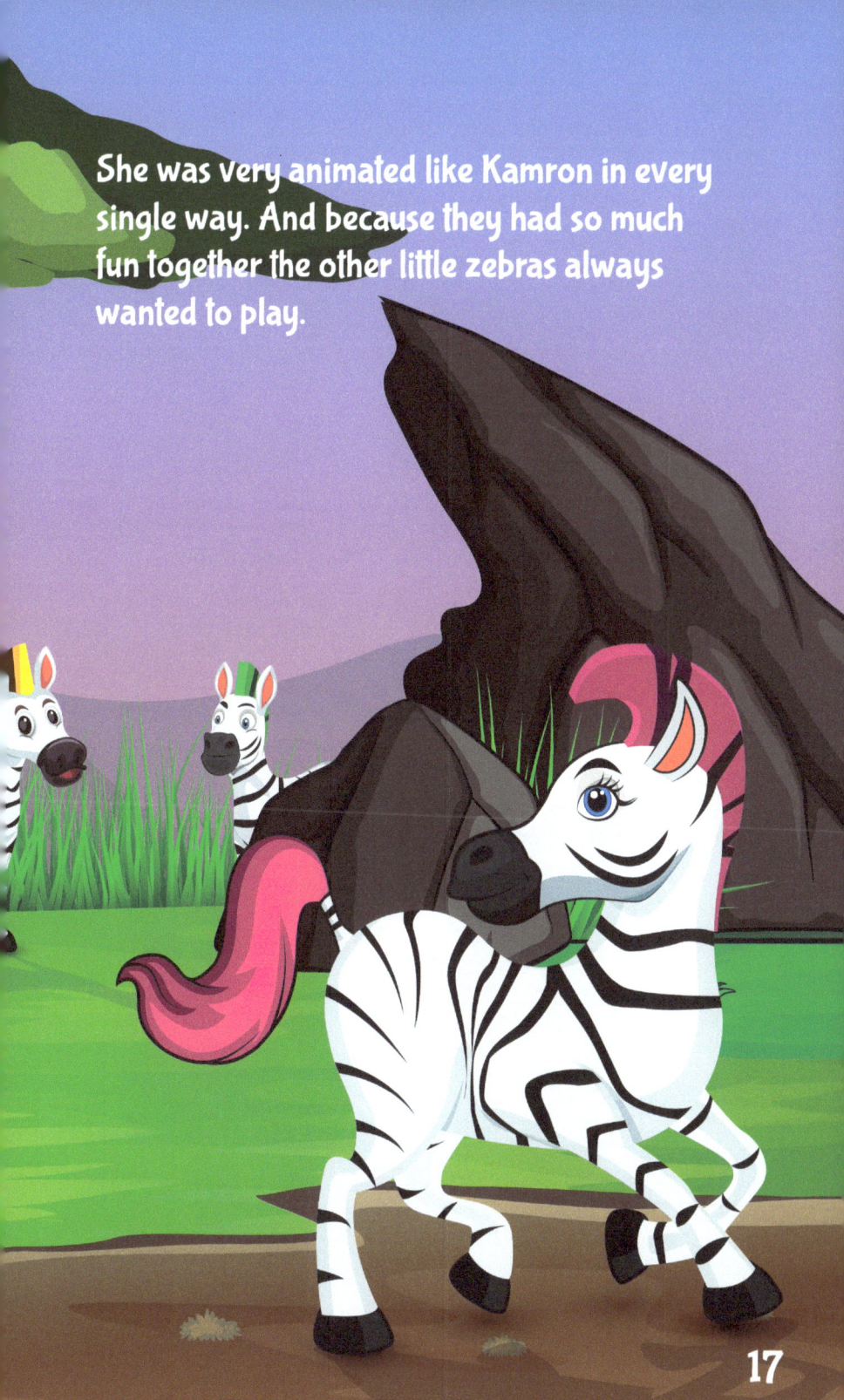

She was very animated like Kamron in every single way. And because they had so much fun together the other little zebras always wanted to play.

They didn't always remember the other zebras names but that was okay because they remembered them by mane.

And when one got really upset,
the other knew just what to do.

Together they would count backwards, take walks or have a snack or two.

And when others try to make you feel a little out of place or bizarre,

try to find friends who accept you for who you are.

For more information visit:

- https://www.cdc.gov/ncbddd/adhd/links.html

- https://www.helpguide.org/articles/add-adhd/when-your-child-has-attention-deficit-disorder-adhd.htm

- https://www.healthline.com/health/adhd/parenting-tips#behavior-management

ADHD Parenting Tips:

- Exercising is great for burning off excess energy, stimulating the brain and helps with concentration.

- Give rewards or praises when noticing positive behavior traits. Giving rewards or praises teaches children what behaviors are desired and acceptable.

- Provide a daily routine that is easy to adapt to. This will create structure and lessen stress and possible meltdowns.

- Create good sleeping habits to increase their mood and energy levels.

- Simplify your request. Giving your child smaller duties will decrease their anxiety about complex tasks.

- Positivity is key! A child with ADHD may often face daily criticism. Staying positive can help build their confidence and create positive self awareness.